Little, Brown and Company

Hachette Book Group
237 Park Avenue, New York, NY 10017
Visit our website at lb-kids.com

Little, Brown and Company is a division of Hachette Book Group, Inc.
The Little, Brown name and logo are trademarks of Hachette Book Group, Inc.

The publisher is not responsible for websites (or their content) that are not owned by the publisher.

First Edition: September 2014

ISBN 978-0-316-25750-3

Library of Congress Control Number: 2014940696

10 9 8 7 6 5 4 3 2 1

WOR

Printed in the United States of America

Dear Patrick,

It has been a joy to see you grow up so far. I can't wait to see what magnificent things you will do in life. You will always hold a very special place in my heart. Thanks for always being a great little boy and big brother.

Much love,

Gracie

# THE BOXTROLLS

## The Movie Storybook

Adapted by Kirsten Mayer

Screenplay by Irena Brignull & Adam Pava

Based upon the book *Here Be Monsters* by Alan Snow

Little, Brown and Company

New York   Boston

There once was a town named Cheesebridge, and the people there lived for one thing—cheese.

A certain gentleman named Lord Portley-Rind was head of the Cheese Guild. The Cheese Guild was a club for people who loved cheese. And they *really* loved it. They loved white, yellow, and blue cheese. Smoked, creamy, and moldy cheese. Sweet, sharp, and sour cheese—and even cheese that tasted like dirty socks.

Lord Portley-Rind had a daughter named Winnie. She liked cheese, but she didn't love it. She was far more interested in Boxtrolls. In fact, Winnie dreamed of seeing Boxtrolls with her own eyes. She thought she had seen them…but they darted into the shadows before she could be sure. One night, she even thought she saw a boy with the Boxtrolls! He must have been kidnapped, she decided.

You see, every night in Cheesebridge, the lights went out, the people stayed home, and a man named Archibald Snatcher roamed the streets, keeping an eye out for monsters.

"Hide your cheese! Hide your babies! Beware the bloodthirsty monsters!" he shouted.

Years ago, a baby named Trubshaw disappeared from Cheesebridge, and Snatcher claimed that the Boxtrolls were to blame. He *also* said that the creatures would steal their cheese next! "Prepare to say bye-bye to your Brie, cheerio to your cheddar, good-bye to your Gorgonzola," warned Snatcher.

That was how Snatcher had gotten his job as the Boxtroll exterminator in town. A missing baby was one thing, but stolen Gouda was another. If Snatcher caught all the Boxtrolls, he would get to join the Cheese Guild. Snatcher *loved* cheese.

What are Boxtrolls?

The Boxtrolls were gentle creatures who really did not deserve their terrifying reputation. They lived underneath Cheesebridge and, at night, came out of various holes around town. But all they did was pick through trash for discarded treasures. The truth was, they had never stolen a baby—or anyone's cheese.

7

The Boxtrolls took the treasures they found back to their cave to tinker with, and they used them to build marvelous contraptions. They built conveyor belts and music machines, waterwheels and power generators. They were quite dexterous for creatures with only four fingers on each hand.

One of the creatures in the cave had five fingers on each hand—a boy. He had no idea he was a boy, of course. He assumed he was a Boxtroll because he had lived with them from babyhood.

His name was Eggs. You might think he was named after food, but that was not true. He was named after his box.

See, Boxtrolls didn't wear clothing so much as they wore old, discarded boxes. Their names came from what the labels on the boxes read.

Living as a Boxtroll meant that Eggs hadn't really spent any time with other humans, and he hadn't spent much time in the sun, either. He was curious about the people who lived aboveground. And he was more curious about who had been snatching Boxtrolls.

Each year, the people of Cheesebridge celebrated Trubshaw Baby Day. They ate cheese, had a parade, and put on a show in the middle of town. It was a strange way to remember a missing baby.

It just so happened that this particular year, Eggs decided to put on a disguise and sneak around town that very day.

Up on a stage, a woman was entertaining the crowd with a song: *"Trubshaw Senior loved his kid, the same as regular fathers did. If you don't want to share his plight, make sure that you are locked up tight—from Boxtrolls!"*

Eggs couldn't understand. Everyone seemed to be *afraid* of Boxtrolls.

Winnie was also at the show. When she spotted Eggs on the street, she thought she recognized him.

"You were with the Boxtrolls last night," she accused.

"Yes," said Eggs.

"I knew it! I knew it! I knew it!" cried Winnie. "How did you escape?"

"We went underground and—"

"Did they drag you down to their hideous cave?" interrupted Winnie with excitement.

"Huh?" asked Eggs. He was confused. This girl didn't know anything. He took off down the street.

"Come back here!" cried Winnie. "Tell me everything!"

Winnie followed Eggs on his aboveground adventure, and she eventually ended up landing smack on her bottom in the Boxtroll cave—surrounded by its residents!

"Help!" she screamed. "Wealthy girl in danger!"

But none of the Boxtrolls approached her. No one tried to drag her off or bite her. In fact, *they* seemed scared of *her*. And Eggs seemed to be having a conversation with them.

"What's going on?" she asked. "You're not one of them; you're a boy!"

"No, I'm not. I'm a Boxtroll. Eggs the Boxtroll."

"Oh, really?" said Winnie with doubt. "Your ears aren't pointy."
Eggs tugged his ear. "I slept on them funny."
"Give me your hand," she demanded, and she held up Eggs's
hand to one of the Boxtrolls' hand. They looked very different.
Then she held up Eggs's hand to her own. They looked very
similar, even if Eggs's hand was much dirtier.
"See? You're not like them. You're one of us. You're a boy,
Eggs. Or should I call you...the Trubshaw Baby!"

Eggs looked around at his Boxtroll family. "I'm a Boxtroll, aren't I?" The Boxtrolls shook their heads, and then they burbled and gurgled a sad story about how a baby was given to them to care for, to keep away from Snatcher. Ever since then, Snatcher had been hunting the Boxtrolls and, well, snatching them.

Winnie and Eggs realized that Snatcher had made up the whole story about the Boxtrolls' stealing a baby so he could set himself up with a job as the Boxtroll exterminator and get into the Cheese Guild. It had all been for the cheese!

"We can tell your father I'm the Trubshaw Baby,"
Eggs told Winnie. "And he'll stop Snatcher!"

"If I agree to help, you have to do exactly as I say."

"I promise," said Eggs.

Then Winnie asked the Boxtrolls to bring her all
sorts of treasures—fabric, thread, ribbons, and more—
and together they made Eggs a new outfit. "Now you
look like a proper boy." Winnie nodded in satisfaction.
"Come on, Eggs."

17

Winnie took Eggs to a party at her house. Her father hosted the entire Cheese
Guild every year on Trubshaw Baby Day.

The ladies and gentlemen of Cheesebridge were delicately nibbling on
Roquefort and Camembert. Eggs had only ever eaten bugs before, so he wasn't
exactly sure what to do. Winnie had just told him to say, "Pleased to meet you."

He figured if everyone else was eating cheese, he should, too. Eggs crammed cheese into his mouth with his fingers until his cheeks puffed out. Then he realized a lady was tapping her fork against her plate as a signal. *Aha! Cheese should be eaten with a fork!*

Eggs spit the cheese out and then used a fork to slowly put it back into his mouth. The lady fainted.

Just then, a butler appeared. He announced, "Ladies and gentlemen, Lord Portley-Rind."

The host appeared and addressed the crowd. "Distinguished members of the Cheese Guild." He then pulled a large sheet off a huge wheel of cheese and pronounced, "I give you the Briehemoth!" The crowd gasped in delight.

Eggs and Winnie tried to reach Lord Portley-Rind, crawling and dodging and jumping around guests. But when Eggs finally reached him, he fell into the wheel of cheese! The Briehemoth rolled—*bump, bump, bump*—down the stairs, out the door, and into the river.

"*Nooooooooooo!*" cried Lord Portley-Rind. "What have you done?"

"Lord Winnie's father?" pleaded Eggs. "People of the upper world? Archibald Snatcher has lied to you all! He told you that Boxtrolls are monsters, that they steal children, but they don't! They would never hurt anyone. I know, because"—he took a deep breath—"I am...the Trubshaw Baby!"

There was silence while everyone waited to see what Lord Portley-Rind would say.

"Do you know how expensive that cheese was?" he asked.

Winnie shouted, "Did you hear a word he said?"

The crowd started whispering among themselves. Snatcher lied! Could it be? Could Eggs be the missing child?

It took some convincing. Boxtrolls ran around without their boxes. Townsfolk screamed. A giant mechanical drill destroyed the Briehemoth after it was fished out of the river. And Snatcher was finally squelched in a giant puddle of melted Brie.

After all that, the townspeople of Cheesebridge realized that the Boxtrolls did not steal babies, and they were not going to steal cheese.

Things slowly got back to normal. Eggs and Winnie helped the Boxtrolls start a recycling business in town.

And all was well. Whether people preferred cheese or bugs for dinner, they could finally eat in peace.

# The End